AMERICAN ELVES - THE YANKOOS

THE YANKOOS AND

LIFE IN THE SONORAN DESERT

BOOK ONE

By Robert Frieders, Ph.D.

One of a Yankoo Series of Books

COVER: This Desert Tortoise is up and about today.
It has left its burrow and is foraging for food.
Notice how the tortoise walks. The legs hold
the tortoise body well above the ground.
Photo by Arizona Game and Fish Department

Yankoo Publishing Co.

AMERICAN ELVES - THE YANKOOS

THE YANKOOS AND

LIFE IN THE SONORAN DESERT

BOOK ONE

By Robert Frieders, Ph.D.

All photographs and line drawings by the author unless indicated otherwise.

Published by: The Yankoo Publishing Co.
10616 W. Cameo Drive
Sun City, Az 85351-2708

First Printing l998

Printed in the United States of America

Library of Congress Catalog Card Number : 98-61677

ISBN 0-9639284-6-5

Acknowledgments

I wish to thank my wife, Dottie, and all our friends who have helped make this book a reality.

Dr. Mamie Ross, Consultant
Professor Marge Edwards, Editor

I am also grateful to the following who have allowed me to use their photos of the Sonoran Desert animals for this book.

Earle A. Robinson
George Olin
Arizona Game and Fish Dept.

We are grateful to our many readers who have been so complimentary of our series on the Oak-Hickory Forest. It is our hope that each of our readers will become the "Friend" that Roscoe guides through our desert. As you travel with Ranger Roscoe, we hope you increase your appreciation of plant and animal life in our Sonoran Desert.
ENJOY YOUR TRIP!

TABLE OF CONTENTS

Chapter	Title	Page

Chapter	Title	Page
1	Roscoe and the Desert Yankoos	5
2	Cactus Pete and the Saguaro	15
3	Abner and the Woodpeckers	27
4	Gilroy and the Grasshoppers	33
5	Percy and the Hedgehog Cactus	41
6	Roscoe and the Woodrat	47
7	Abner and the Cactus Wren	53
8	Roscoe and the Brittlebush	59
9	Horatio and the Yucca Plants	65
10	Creosote Charlie and the Blacktail Jackrabbit	71
11	Ebenezer and the Desert Tortoise	81
12	Cactus Pete and the Beavertail Cactus	87
13	Horatio and Phainopepla and Mistletoe	97
14	Creosote Charlie and the Diamondback Rattlesnake	107
15	Roscoe and the Roundtail Ground Squirrel	113
16	Ebenezer and the Horned Lizard	117
17	Gilroy and the Pipevine Butterfly	123
18	The Creosote Bush	129
19	The Ants	139

CHAPTER ONE
ROSCOE AND THE DESERT YANKOOS

Hello, my friend! Glad to meet you. My name is Roscoe. I am a Yankoo, an American elf. I live out here in the desert. See my hat. It has the words "Ranger Roscoe" on it. Yes, that's me! I am Roscoe, the desert ranger.

Notice my shoulder patch. All desert rangers have this official shoulder patch. It identifies one as a desert ranger. The patch shows a tall cactus plant. That plant is a Saguaro Cactus. We will see many of these tree-like cacti.

6 AMERICAN ELVES - THE YANKOOS

A ranger must be able to answer many questions. What kinds of plants live in the desert? Deserts don't receive much rain. How can plants live with little rain water? How can animals live daily under that hot sun? Do desert plants and animals need one another? These are just a few questions. Rangers must be able to answer these and many more. I wanted to become a ranger, so I knew I had to study. I read many books telling about desert life.

Many days I stayed in the desert. I observed plants and animals there. I learned much about the desert from others. My friend, in all these ways, one learns. After much study, I became a desert ranger. Now my friend, I can tell others about our wonderful desert.

Every day, I travel through our desert. I serve as a guide for persons like you. So, come with me. We shall travel together. In our travels, we will see other Yankoos. You will enjoy meeting these Yankoos. Each is an expert on some aspect of desert life.

Here are some sketches of these Yankoos.

This is a picture of Cactus Pete. He can tell you the name of many a cactus. He has observed and studied their "life styles". He can explain how cacti cope with desert weather.

We will also meet Otis and Oswald.

Otis and Oswald are identical twins. They are miners. They mine for gold in our desert. They will describe how gold was mined at the old Vulture Gold Mine.

8 <u>AMERICAN ELVES - THE YANKOOS</u>

Gilroy is an expert on the desert insects. There are some very beautiful butterflies in our desert. The Giant Swallowtail is one of our desert butterflies. Gilroy will tell you about these and other insects.

Percy is the Yankoo flower expert. He will tell you how all flowers are different. Yet, in essence, they are all very much alike. Percy will tell you about our desert flowers.

Horatio is the desert ecologist. He studies how plants and animals need one another. You will be amazed at how each helps the other.

Abner edits our Yankoo Gazette. It is our desert newspaper. Abner is also the Yankoo expert on desert birds. We have many different kinds of birds in our desert.

Ebenezer is our "rock hound". He is forever looking for new rocks and stones. He has spent much time observing our desert lizards. He will tell you about them.

We must not forget our Yankoo cowboy, Creosote Charlie. He captures and rides those big jackrabbits. As you would expect, Charlie is an expert on rabbits and snakes.

Those are the Yankoos you will meet in our travels.

Now, let me show you where our desert is located.
Let me make a sketch for you.

Our desert lies in the southwestern part of the United
States and in Mexico. Below these states, I made a
thick line. That is the boundary line between the
United States and Mexico. One area in Mexico is called
Sonora. Notice that. Part of Mexico extends down
from California. It is called Baha California.

Now, I will sketch in the desert area on this map.

As you can see, much of this desert lies in Mexico. It covers almost all of the area called Sonora. That is why the desert was named the Sonoran Desert. Much of the Sonoran Desert in the United States lies in the state of Arizona. In our travels, we will spend time in various Arizona parts of the Sonoran Desert.

Before we head out, let's check the weather forecast for today. Notice that large sign over there. The sign gives the weather forecast for desert travelers.

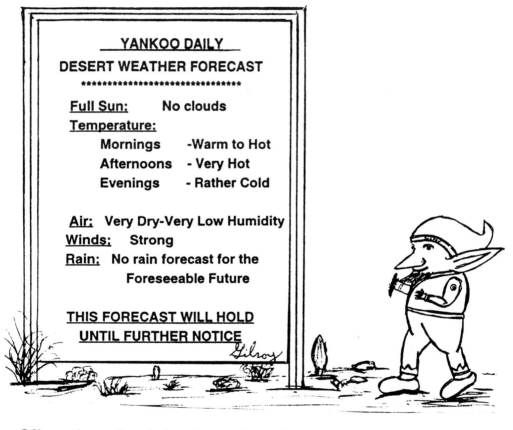

YANKOO DAILY
DESERT WEATHER FORECAST
****

Full Sun: No clouds
Temperature:
     Mornings   -Warm to Hot
     Afternoons   - Very Hot
     Evenings   - Rather Cold

Air: Very Dry-Very Low Humidity
Winds: Strong
Rain: No rain forecast for the
     Foreseeable Future

THIS FORECAST WILL HOLD
UNTIL FURTHER NOTICE
Gilroy

Gilroy has the job of posting desert weather forecasts. It is an easy job. Our Sonoran Desert has several rainfalls each year. When the winter and summer rains are due, Gilroy changes the forecast on that sign. Otherwise, the forecast you see there holds. Every day is much the same.

The sun shines down. It heats up the ground. It heats up the air above the ground. It's a wonder plants do not burn up. They don't. They "keep their cool". All desert plants and animals have developed ways to "beat the heat". Desert air is so very dry. There is very little moisture in the air. This has a drying effect on desert plants and animals. The strong desert winds make this even worse. It's a wonder plants don't dry up. They don't. They know how to handle this desert weather. The same holds true for the animals. It is dry and hot every day. Why don't desert animals die of thirst? Well, desert animals don't die from lack of water. Each animal, in its own way, has solved the desert "water problem". We shall learn much more about the weather and desert life in our travels.

Before we start, I must check my list. I have told you the name of our desert. You now know where it is located. We talked a little about the weather. Yes, we also took note of Gilroy's weather forecast. I also told you about our desert Yankoos. You will enjoy meeting them.

Here is a picture we took at our reunion last year. Not all of our desert Yankoos were there.

Now, let's head out into the Sonoran Desert.

CHAPTER TWO
CACTUS PETE AND THE SAGUARO

Look, there's Cactus Pete by that tall cactus. Hi, Cactus Pete! Hi, Roscoe! Hello, my friend. I see Ranger Roscoe is guiding you through our desert.

Cactus Pete, perhaps you could tell our friend about this tall cactus. Oh, I would be happy to do that, Roscoe.

That, my friend, is a Saguaro Cactus. It's a tall, green plant.

The Saguaro is a tree-like cactus. It is all trunk. It has no leaves. Notice its shape. The cactus is round. It swells out in the middle, doesn't it? It is not as round at the top and the base, is it? Notice, that cactus has pleats - folds.

Imagine that I have taken a slice out of that cactus. This slice, called a cross section, would look like this.

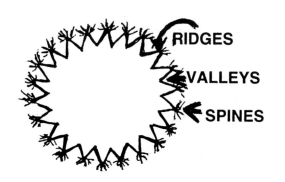

RIDGES

VALLEYS

SPINES

See how it is pleated. It has deep valleys and high ridges. Long sharp spines come off those ridges.

Inside every Saguaro is a skeleton. The skeleton holds the cactus up in the air. See, over there is a skeleton. It stands straight up. That was a living cactus once. It was like those you see back towards the hill. Then, the cactus died. All that is left now is the skeleton.

The skeleton looks like a bunch of long sticks, doesn't it? Well, those long sticks are called ribs. They are hard and woody. The ribs are arranged in a circle. The ribs are connected at the base.

They are also connected where the arm comes off. In the main trunk, the ribs are not connected. They are independent. Here and there, one or the other might be connected. But most are not joined. Notice how the top looks like a circle of loose ribs.

The cactus is anchored in the soil by roots. These roots hold the tall cactus up in the air. A strong tap root comes off the base of the cactus. This tap root grows straight down. Thick side roots branch off this tap root. There are also many small roots. These lie close to the surface. Let me make a sketch. Say we have a Saguaro that is ten feet tall.

10 FEET

10 FEET

The small rootlets would extend outwards about ten feet.

Here, I will make another sketch. It will show the same thing. Say we are up in the air. We look down on the cactus. Notice the cactus trunk has two arms. They are in the center of the sketch. Branching outwards about ten feet are many, many rootlets. They extend out as far as the height of the cactus. These rootlets connect with the tap root.

10 FEET

CACTUS TRUNK + TWO ARMS
LOOKING DOWN ON CACTUS

The Saguaro cactus, my friend, has an interesting water system. Let me tell you how it works. Say we have a summer thunderstorm. I will sketch this.

Much rain falls. Sheets of water move over the ground. The upper part of the soil becomes soaked with water. The rootlets there now act like sponges. They quickly take in this water. The rootlets then act like "pipes". They move the water down to the tap root area. The water is then taken up into the main trunk. The water is stored there in live cells.

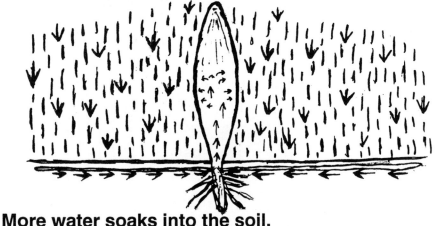

More water soaks into the soil.

Rootlets absorb this additional water. The water in the rootlets moves down to the tap root area. Up it goes into the trunk. There, it is also stored in live cells. As this continues, the main trunk expands; it becomes "fatter". The ribs move farther apart. The new rib position now supports the enlarged and heavier trunk.

Here is a drawing of the trunk. It is a side view of the trunk. It shows the rib locations in rainy weather and during dry, hot periods.

RAINY WEATHER
Water from the rain is stored in live cells.

Ribs move farther apart to hold new weight.
HAPPENS QUICKLY!

DRY, HOT DAYS
Water is used in living and growing.

Ribs move closer together.
HAPPENS SLOWLY!

Here is a cross section view of the trunk. It shows rib and outside "skin" views in rainy weather and in a hot, dry, drought period.

RAINY WEATHER
Water from the rain is stored in live cells.

Ribs move farther apart to hold up the new weight.

Outside folds flatten out.
Cactus gets "fatter"
HAPPENS QUICKLY!

DRY, HOT DAYS
Water is used in living and growing.

Ribs move closer together.

Outside folds move closer together.
Cactus gets "thinner".
HAPPENS SLOWLY!

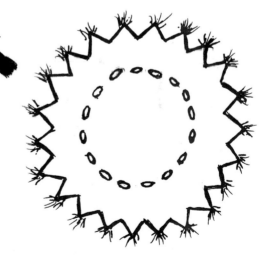

What do you think of that water tank, my friend? It is adjustable. Our desert receives just two rainy periods a year, at most. The Saguaro must store as much water as possible when it rains. It quickly takes up this water.

The Saguaro stores the water in cells in the trunk. The trunk of the cactus gets rounder, "fatter". It "bellies out" in a hurry. Then come the dry, hot days of the rest of the year. To live and grow, the Saguaro uses water from this tank. During this drought period, it slowly contracts. It gets thinner; it "slims down". My friend, that water tank adjusts its size to the amount of water it holds. That is a marvel of nature. It is an engineering feat!

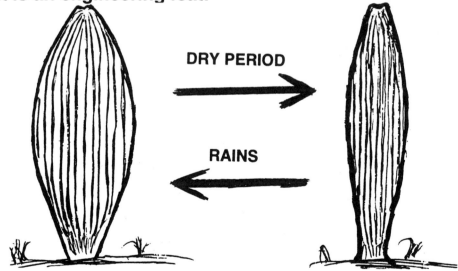

DRY PERIOD

RAINS

In addition, the cactus loses little water to the dry air. It is covered with a wax coat. This wax coat reduces water loss. This is one desert plant that doesn't worry about water. The dry periods can come. They can last for a long time. The Saguaro has enough water to go on living.

Most days, my friend, are all alike in our desert. The sun's rays make sure it is a hot, dry day. How can the Saguaro stand this daily hot weather? Let me explain how it has adapted to this desert weather. Here is a sketch of a Saguaro Cactus.

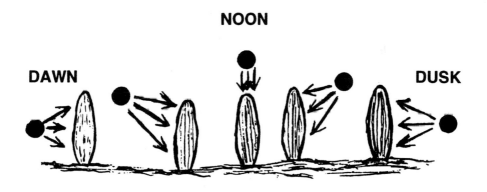

The sun shines on that cactus from dawn to dusk. One can see how important the round, tall shape of that cactus is. The cactus shape determines how much sunlight each area receives. During the day, all areas receive sunlight. How much depends on the time of day. No single area of the cactus receives the full impact of the sun's rays all day. In addition, some of this sunlight is reflected back into the air. The Saguaro has many spines. These spines reflect rays of the sun. The spines also cast a shadow on the cactus trunk. The cactus benefits from this shade.

Look at the shadows those spines cast. Many spines line the ridges of the cactus trunk. The spines are arranged in clumps of from fifteen to thirty spines. The clusters are spaced an inch apart. Spines shade the plant even while the sun's rays shine on it.

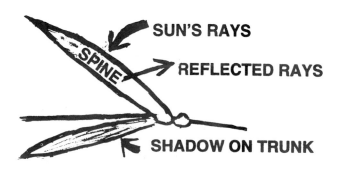

SUN'S RAYS

SPINE

REFLECTED RAYS

SHADOW ON TRUNK

The spines shield a large area from the sun.

In all these ways, the Saguaro "beats the desert heat". In spite of the hot, dry days, the Saguaro remains cooler than the air around it. Inside, the cactus is about ten degrees cooler than the air outside.

Spines also protect the cactus. Faced with those spines, few animals try taking a bite. Spines toward the top are lighter in color and flexible. Farther down, the spines are darker and brittle.

Our desert winds are often strong and very dry. Winds sweep over the flat landscape. The tall Saguaro is buffeted by these winds. How does it manage to keep standing? Well, the Saguaro has also solved the desert "wind problem". Consider the Saguaro's shape. It is a round structure. Winds blow; they strike the cactus. Winds are deflected around it. Being round reduces the full force of the wind.

W
I
N
D

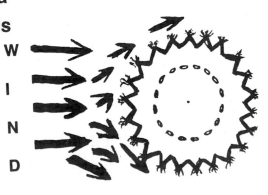

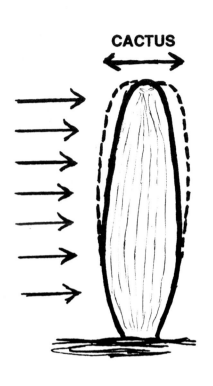

CACTUS

One other cactus feature helps when the wind blows. Recall, inside the trunk is a circle of ribs. These ribs are flexible. They give a little in the wind. They let the cactus sway a little in a strong wind. If this did not happen, winds would probably topple it.

That Saguaro is designed for desert living. It has solved desert weather problems; little water, high temperature, strong winds. It goes on living in spite of the desert weather conditions.

My friend, enjoy your travel with Roscoe. I must be off. Later, I will tell you much more about that Saguaro cactus. Goodbye, Roscoe!
Goodbye, Cactus Pete!

CHAPTER THREE
ABNER AND THE WOODPECKERS

Hi, Abner! Hi, Roscoe!
I'm watching woodpeckers.
Look at the holes
in that cactus.

Two kinds
of birds
made the
holes.
This Gilded
Flicker
made one.
Notice its
black,
spotted
breast. It
has a red
moustache.
See it there.

Photo by Earle A. Robinson

The Gilded Flicker makes its nest in the upper trunk of the Saguaro. It is a large bird. It needs a large nest. High on the cactus, it cuts out an opening. Then, it digs out the wet pulpy material. The weak, thin ribs up there are in the way. So, it cuts through those ribs.

A large area inside is excavated for the nest. The nest walls become covered with a gummy sap. This dries and becomes thick scar tissue. This covering reduces infection from air microbes. It also prevents water loss from the cactus. The pair of flickers will raise their young in this nest.

Flickers are ground-feeding birds. They have a slim pointed bill. They also have a long tongue. These are ideal for capturing ants and ground insects.

The Gila Woodpecker makes the other hole in the Saguaro. Look at this picture. Notice that the male

has a round, red cap.
It has "zebra-like" stripes on its wings.
The Gila Woodpecker is smaller than the GIlded Flicker.
It needs a smaller nest. It makes this nest down farther on the cactus trunk. Here

Photo by Earle A. Robinson

the cactus is rounder. With its bill, it cuts a hole.
The bill breaks off sharp ends of spines by the hole.

The Gila Woodpecker digs out the wet pulp material. It excavates a space that goes back to the strong woody ribs. It does not cut through these ribs. As with the Gilded Flicker, the excavated area walls become covered with a gummy sap. This dries and becomes a hard covering all around the nest space. The female lays eggs in this nest. The pair takes turns incubating the eggs. When the young are born the woodpeckers are kept busy hunting for food. These woodpeckers seek insects living on desert plants. They dig out insect larvae tunneling in cactus plants. They also eat mistletoe berries and cactus fruits.

Both the Gilded Flicker and the Gila Woodpecker make new nests every year. Other desert birds take over the old nesting sites.

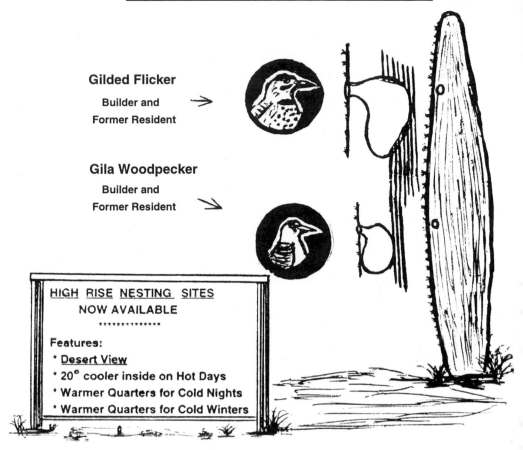

Gilded Flicker

Builder and
Former Resident

Gila Woodpecker

Builder and
Former Resident

HIGH RISE NESTING SITES
NOW AVAILABLE
* * * * * * * * * * * * * *

Features:
* Desert View
* 20° cooler inside on Hot Days
* Warmer Quarters for Cold Nights
* Warmer Quarters for Cold Winters

A few of the possible new residents.

Purple Martin

Sparrow Hawk

Screech Owl

Elf Owl

Crested Flycatcher

When the Saguaro dies, the soft tissues break down quickly. It is then that one finds the hard woody ribs. One can also find a "boot" at this time. The "boot" is the name given that hard covering around the nest area. See, here is a boot by this Saguaro.

Here is a close up of a "boot". It came from a Gila Woodpecker nest.

CHAPTER FOUR
GILROY AND THE GRASSHOPPERS

We certainly scared up some
grasshoppers, didn't we, my
friend. Let's find one on the
ground. They certainly are
hard to see against this gravelly ground.

Oh, look. Gilroy is over there. Hi, Gilroy! Hi, Roscoe!

Gilroy, we can't find a grasshopper on the ground.
Will you help us?   I'll be right over, Roscoe. Glad to
meet you, my friend. Now, let's find a hopper for you.

Why, there it is. Notice the shadow it casts on the ground. That is a Pallid-winged Grasshopper.

My friend, you have now seen one of the most common insects in our desert. Notice how it blends in with the ground.Its color protects it on that ground. Many an animal would overlook it there. However, to stay alive, the grasshopper must not move. Once it moves, a nearby animal would quickly spot it.

Many, many grasshoppers are produced each year. Many wil reproduce. They will provide eggs for next year's grasshoppers. Female grasshoppers lay many eggs in their lifetime.

Eggs are deposited in a hole in the ground. The female grasshopper digs a hole in the ground. In making this hole, no dirt is removed. Yet, a hole is made in the ground. My friend, I can't do this. Say I dig a hole in the ground. To make the hole, I remove some dirt. The female grasshopper digs a hole in the ground. In doing so, it removes no dirt. Let me make a drawing showing how this is done.

The female has two moveable prongs on its rear end. With the prongs closed, it pushes down into the dirt. Then, it expands the prongs. This compresses the dirt outwards. It continues going deeper and deeper.

With the hole at the right depth, it lays eggs. It pours a glue-like material over the egg mass. This material dries and hardens. The frothy material has many openings and cavities. This allows air into the eggs. It also provides air for the young grasshoppers that hatch.

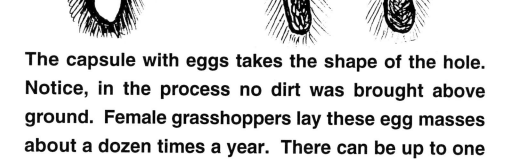

The capsule with eggs takes the shape of the hole. Notice, in the process no dirt was brought above ground. Female grasshoppers lay these egg masses about a dozen times a year. There can be up to one hundred eggs in each capsule.

The following spring, the eggs will hatch. Out come very small grasshoppers. Each has a large head. The young can walk and hop with their legs. They have no wings.

As they grow in size, a wing bud appears on each side of the back. These gradually grow into mature wings. Once the grasshopper reaches full size, it is mature. It walks; it flies; it hops; - and can it jump!

WING BUD

Many grasshoppers produced every year become food for other animals. My friend, here are two words we use often. An animal that hunts another animal is called a <u>predator.</u> The animal that is hunted is called the <u>prey</u>. A bird capturing a grasshopper is the predator. The grasshopper is the prey. Grasshoppers have to watch out for many predators. Many grasshoppers will be eaten. Grasshoppers try their best not to be eaten. Catching a grasshopper is not an easy task. A predator cannot sneak up on a grasshopper. No way! The grasshopper sees the predator coming.

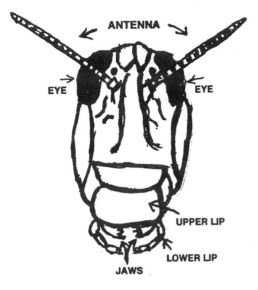

Grasshoppers have two big eyes on their heads. The large eyes bring in images of everything around the grasshopper. The right eye brings in the view on the right side. The left eye registers the view on the left side. Both eyes see toward the front and the rear.

Both eyes also pick up anything in the air above. So a predator cannot sneak up on a grasshopper. The grasshopper sees it coming. In a split-second before it is caught, off goes the grasshopper. It puts some distance between it and the

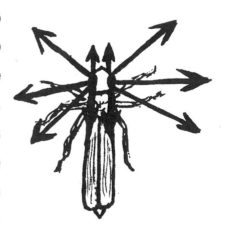

predator. If a greater distance is needed, it flies away. If a shorter distance would suffice, it makes a big jump. Now, the predator might not even know where it landed! So, catching a grasshopper is not an easy task.

Grasshoppers can really jump, my friend. A grasshopper is only one and one-half inches long. It can make a horizontal leap of thirty inches. That is a jump twenty times its length. I am one and one-half

foot tall. To do what the grasshopper does, I would have to jump twenty times my height. I would have to make a thirty-foot jump. No way could I compete in jumping with a grasshopper.

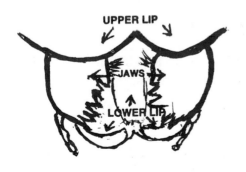

UPPER LIP

JAWS

LOWER LIP

Grasshoppers have very strong teeth. The teeth move sideways as in this sketch. Grasshoppers can eat most any plant in the desert.

They have an upper lip. They also have a lower lip. Then there are those two jaws. These are strong chewing teeth. Plant material is chewed and crushed into small pieces. Then, it is swallowed.

What was that, my friend? Oh, you wonder how a grasshopper endures standing on the hot desert sand. It solves that problem easily.

If the ground is too hot, it just extends its legs. Now, it is farther away from the hot ground. Breezes can move underneath it.   If it is still too hot, the grasshopper takes to the air. It is cooler there. It usually heads for the shade. It rests behind a rock under a tree or a bush. Those grasshoppers will keep cool, one way or another.

Here is a mouse. It is a Grasshopper Mouse. It eats grasshoppers.

Well, let's be on our way. Thanks, Gilroy, for the help in finding that grasshopper. We also learned much about the grasshopper from you.   Goodbye, Gilroy! Goodbye, Roscoe!   Goodbye, my friend!

CHAPTER FIVE
PERCY AND THE HEDGEHOG CACTUS

Hi, Roscoe! I'm surprised to see you in this part of the desert today. Hi, Percy! We're looking at these cacti here, Percy. Would you tell my friend about these Hedgehog Cacti? I'll be happy to do that Roscoe.

The Hedgehog Cactus has a water system like the Saguaro Cactus system. The stems are covered by a pleated outside layer. The ridges move farther apart as water is stored in the round stems. The ridges move closer together as water is used in living and growing. So, the Hedgehog Cactus also has an adjustable water tank. During long dry periods, the Hedgehog Cactus uses the water stored in its tank.

The Hedgehog Cactus blooms in the springtime. It blooms here in March and April.

Here is a Hedgehog Cactus in bloom. A number of flowers are in full bloom. Some are just opening. Others will be blooming shortly. Each flower will open for several days. Notice that the flower is cup-shaped. The flower's color advertises for the plant. It attracts bees and other insects. The insects will pollinate the flower. No seeds will be produced unless the flower is pollinated.

All flowers have similar parts. Here, I will sketch a side view of a flower.

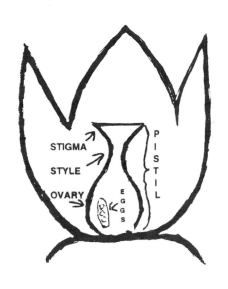

The center part is called the PISTIL. Each part of the PISTIL has a name. The top part is called a stigma. The long thin part is called the style. The bottom part is called the ovary. Eggs are produced in the ovary. If the flower is pollinated, these eggs will develop into seeds.

Flowers have one other structure. It is called the STAMEN. The top of the stamen is called the anther. The anther is held up by a long thin structure called a filament. The anther produces pollen grains. Flowers usually have many STAMENS. Flowers usually have one central PISTIL.

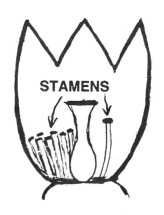

Now you know the parts of a flower, my friend. The Hedgehog Cactus shows these flower parts. Here is a single Hedgehog Cactus flower.

The pistil is in the center. The top of the pistil is the stigma. It is green in color.   In this flower, the stigma has a number of branches. All the whitish dots in the flower are the anthers, the top of the stamens. These anthers produce mature pollen grains.

Let me explain how this Hedgehog Cactus is pollinated. First, let's make a few sketches.

A bee notices the flower. It flies toward the flower. The stigma of the flower is much higher than the many stamens. The stigma is also wider. It is an ideal landing spot. The bee lands on the surface of the stigma. The bee now looks for nectar. Nectar pools usually lie in the bottom part of a flower. So, the bee drops down among the stamens.

The bee brushes up against the stamens while searching for the nectar pools. As it does this, the bee picks up pollen grains. Pollen grains on those anthers are sticky. The pollen grains stick to the hairy bee legs.

Having secured some nectar, the bee flies away from this flower. Now, it flies to another Hedgehog flower.

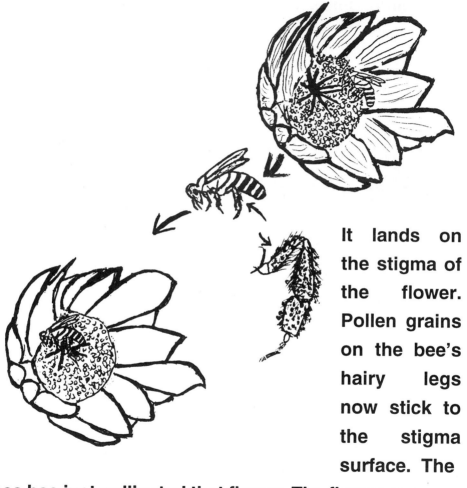

It lands on the stigma of the flower. Pollen grains on the bee's hairy legs now stick to the stigma surface. The bee has just pollinated that flower. The flower can now make seeds. Many seeds become food for desert animals. Some seeds start new Hedgehog Cacti.

Goodbye, Percy! Thanks, we have learned a lot about flowers.

CHAPTER SIX
ROSCOE AND THE WOODRAT

My friend, look over there. Do you see that pile under that tree? That is a Woodrat nest. The animal is also called a Packrat.

Let's get closer to that nest. It is a pile of many, many pieces of a cholla cactus. Why, we just passed a group of cholla cacti. Let's go back there. Look on the ground under those cacti. Those are sections, pieces of cactus. We call these pieces - joints. There are many joints under all those cholla cacti.

This is where the Woodrat secured its nest material. The Woodrat carried all those cholla joints back for its nest. How did the Woodrat do this? Well, I imagine it picked up each joint with its mouth. It probably carried each joint back to the nest in its mouth.

Here is a section of the cholla cactus. Look at those joints. The joints have long sharp spines. Grabbing these joints with its mouth would prove dangerous for an animal. The spines would pierce lips, areas inside the mouth and head areas. The Woodrat probably bites off some spines. It will also eat material inside a joint. So it carries the spiny joint back to its nest.

Let's go back to the nest again.

It's a pile of joints and sticks. Inside this nest is the Woodrat's living area. An old burrow of a ground squirrel makes a cool underground nest. The round living space is lined with soft plant fibers. There are passageways at ground level leading to the living quarters. During the day the Woodrat stays inside this nest. It places cactus joints in openings. The nest provides shade. The Woodrat rests. When night falls, out comes the Woodrat. It's time to look for food. It has its favorite trails.

Look, there is a Woodrat. Notice it has large ears. It is walking over those sharp spines of the cholla joints.

Photo by George Olin

Some other animals can also do this. The Cactus Wren, Ground Squirrel, and the White-footed Mouse also walk on these cactus joints. How they do this without being injured is a mystery.

The Woodrat is a plant eater, a herbivore. It forages for food at night. It eats mature and developing pads of prickly pear cacti. In spring it eats developing branches of mesquite and palo verde trees. It also eats grasses and seed pods of trees. When dawn approaches,the Woodrat heads back to its nest.

| Western Diamondback Rattlesnake | Coyote | Great Horned Owl | Gray Fox |

All these predators prey on Woodrats. Few predators would try entering the Woodrat nest. The rattlesnake may make its way in. The snake would probably not find the Woodrat. The nest has emergency exits. The Woodrat would have vanished.

Well, let's be on our way, my friend.

Look at that butterfly, my friend. It is the Painted Lady Butterfly. It is found all year in our Sonoran Desert and the southwest. Every year the southwest Painted Lady butterflies migrate east and north. They migrate all the way up to the subartic in North America. Its migration is essentially one way. Next year, other southwest Painted Ladies will migrate.

The Painted Lady is perhaps the most widespread butterfly in the world. It is found in Europe, Africa, Asia, North America and a number of islands.This has earned it another name - the Cosmopolitan Butterfly.

CHAPTER SEVEN
ABNER AND THE CACTUS WREN

Look, my friend, Abner is over there by those cholla cactus. He sees us. Hi, Abner!

Hi, Roscoe! I see you have found me again today. I usually check in on a family of wrens. They have a nest in this cholla cactus. These cacti are favorite nesting sites for our Cactus Wren.

Look at that bird. It is just leaving its nest. My, friend, that is a Cactus Wren. These wrens are the largest wrens living in North America. Notice, it has a slender, somewhat curved bill.

Photo by Earle A. Robinson

That bird believes in security. That nest is set deep in between those plant sections. All around it are those sharp, long spines. That nest is safe from snakes and many predators.

The Cactus Wren nests in late spring. Like other wrens, the Cactus Wren may make multiple nests. The male makes a loosely constructed nest for roosting. A roosting nest also provides shelter in rainy weather. The female constructs a better nest. Stems of wild buckwheat are used. The nest looks like a bag laid on its side. Grasses and twigs line the tunnel leading in.   Inside, the nest is lined with feathers. The nest is well shaded by cholla joints, spines and grass-twig construction.

Photo by Earle A. Robinson

These birds have young in their nest. Do you see that young bird inside? It is already quite large.

Photo by Earle A. Robinson

Will you look at that, my friend? The parents are both back with food for their young. Feeding hungry mouths each day keeps them busy. Wrens are insect eaters. They go about searching for food very systematically. They look over an area. They flip aside a leaf. They look under things. The favorite hunting area is right under the nest. They search there every day for food.

Cactus Wrens eat ants, wasps, grasshoppers, sow bugs, and spiders. They also eat berries and fruit.

After the young have left the nest, a White-footed Mouse often moves in. Other desert birds also nest in the cholla cacti. Road runners and the Curved-bill Thrasher regularly construct nests there.

My friend, look at the spider on that rock. That is a Wolf Spider. Notice, it has eight legs. All spiders have eight legs. All spiders are predators. They prey on live insects. Live insects are their food.

Most spiders spin webs. They capture live insects, their prey, in their webs. This Wolf Spider does not spin a web. It spends its life on the ground. It forages for prey, live insects, mostly at night. It overtakes and captures insects on the ground. The ends of each leg have three small claws. These help in capturing and holding the insects. My friend, here we have a predator-prey setup in nature. Spiders are the predators. They hunt live insects. Live insects are the prey. Live insects are the spider's food.

CHAPTER EIGHT
ROSCOE AND THE BRITTLEBUSH

Look at those plants there, my friend. Those are Brittlebushes. You know brittle means easily broken. Place a leaf between your fingers. Now, bend it. It will snap in two. So, leaves of these bushes are indeed easily broken. Brittlebushes are common plants in our desert. They grow on rocky slopes. One finds them also on flat plain areas. There are some right there.

Notice those plants. They are low, branching plants. They range in height from two to three feet.

The Brittlebush is a unique plant. It has two different kinds of leaves in a year. One leaf type is suited for the moist period. The second kind of leaf is adapted for the dry period.

The spring rains come. Many new rootlets are made in the soil. They bring in soil water to the plant. The stems begin to lengthen. New leaves are produced on these stems. These leaves are suited for this moist period. The leaves are bluish-green in color. The leaves take in about eighty percent of the sun's rays. With water now available and less heat, the plant grows rapidly. The plant will produce many flowers on long stems above the leaves.

The blooms are about several inches wide.

So many flowers are produced. The flowers cover the plant like a yellow "umbrella".

The flowers are now gone. The long flower stems are still there. These will dry up and fall off the plant.

Now, the desert dry period begins. The Brittlebush adapts. As the soil dries, all those rootlets are not needed. So they are shed. The leaves now are adapted to reflect much of the sun's rays. Whitish-gray leaves are produced.

These leaves are covered with very many fine hairs. These hairs are filled inside with air. This leaf surface now reflects about seventy percent of the sun's rays. The Brittlebush goes on living. However, there is very little new growth.

As the soil becomes very dry, even this plant cannot be maintained. So many of the whitish gray leaves are dropped. Any leaves remaining have the hairs pressed flat against the leaf surface. Often all that remains are the dried out branches. A "skeleton" now waits for spring rains. Given rainy weather from October to January, the plant starts to grow again. Stems grow longer.

They produce new leaves. The new leaves are adapted for this moist period. With enough water the Brittlebush will flower. Once again, the Brittlebush will brighten up our desert landscape with yellow flowers.

Look at those small cacti there, my friend.

This is a dense cluster of Pincushion Cacti. Each plant is about six inches tall.Flowers are formed on the top of the stem. They make a circle - like a crown. The flowers last for several days. They are beautiful.

CHAPTER NINE
HORATIO AND THE YUCCA PLANT

Look over there, my friend. That is Horatio. He is by that Yucca plant.   Hi, Horatio!   Hi, Roscoe! I see you have a friend with you.   Yes, Horatio, my friend is learning about desert life.   Roscoe, I could tell your friend something. It's about this Yucca plant here. That would be fine, Horatio.

My friend,   this is a Yucca plant. All Yuccas have long, sharp-pointed leaves like this plant. All Yuccas have waxy, white flowers.

Look at this flower over here. Notice there are many Yucca moths inside the flower.

Yucca plants have developed a close relationship with these small white moths. The moth is called the Yucca Moth. The Yucca plant and Yucca Moth need one another. The plant provides a place where moths can lay their eggs. It also provides food and shelter for the moth larvae. The Yucca Moth helps the plant. It pollinates the Yucca flowers. Once pollinated by the Yucca Moth, seeds are produced.

Here is a flower of the Yucca. One can clearly see the flower parts.

Horatio, I know what those flower parts are called. You do, my friend. Yes, Percy told me about flower parts. I learned about flowers when we looked at the Hedgehog Cactus flowers.

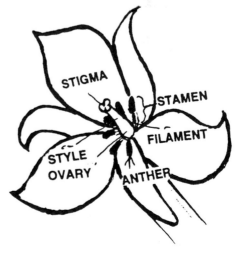

In the center of that flower is the pistil. The top part of the pistil is called the stigma. The middle part is called the style. The bottom part is called the ovary. Egg cells are present in the ovary. Those six parts around the pistil are called stamens. The top part of the stamen is called an anther. It produces the pollen grains. The anthers are held up by thin structures called filaments. Did I get it right, Horatio?

You certainly did, my friend. Now, let me explain how the Yucca plant and the Yucca Moth need one another. When the Yucca flower opens, the moths appear. The males mate with the female moths. A female moth then goes to a Yucca flower. The moth has a specialized beak. It is curved. It uses this to scrape sticky pollen grains on the anther together. It does this on a number of anthers. It now has a rather large sticky ball of pollen grains. It holds it with its curved beak.

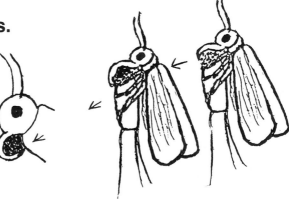

Now the moth flies to another flower.

The moth goes down to the
bottom part of the pistil. With
its posterior, it makes a hole
in the ovary wall. It will then
lay some eggs inside the ovary.

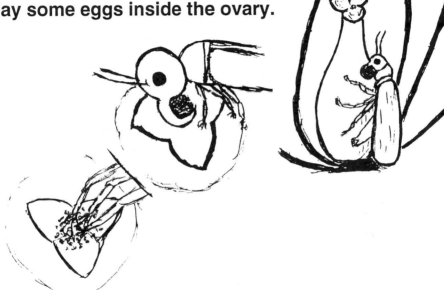

The moth then goes to the stigma of this flower. Here
the moth puts the pollen grains on the stigma surface.
It presses the pollen grains into the stigma surface.
The pollen grains ensure the fertilization of many eggs.
These fertilized eggs will produce seeds. In the
meantime, the Yucca Moth eggs have hatched. The
larvae begin eating Yucca   seeds.

More seeds are produced than the larvae can eat. These will help in starting new Yucca plants. The moth larvae inside the ovary are safe from predators. They will eventually reach a mature size. Once mature, the larvae make a hole in the seed case wall.

See this picture. It shows two openings in the seed case. The larvae made their exit through these openings. Dropping to the ground, each larva changes into a pupa stage. In this stage, the larva will change into a moth. By next year, the change will have been made. When the Yucca flowers open, Yucca Moths will appear. We must be going now. Goodbye, Horatio!   Goodbye, Roscoe !

CHAPTER TEN
THE BLACKTAIL JACKRABBIT

There's Creosote Charlie. Hi, Creosote Charlie! Hi, Roscoe! I have been watching this jackrabbit over here. Let me tell you about it. Look at that Blacktail Jackrabbit. See it standing there by that rock. A bird is also standing next to the jackrabbit. That jackrabbit has long ears, doesn't it? The ears are black on top.

Photo by George Olin

Jackrabbits are much larger than our Cottontail Rabbits. They are also heavier animals. Notice that eye on the left side of the head. It bulges out from the head. Jackrabbits live in open desert areas. They know their home territory very well. Every hideaway has probably been used many times. Each jackrabbit has many resting places. These are called forms. A form is not a burrow. It is a clear area surrounded by grasses or a dense brush thicket. During the day, the jackrabbit sits in the shade of the form. It is cooler there. The thicket gives some relief from those dry, hot desert winds. The forms also provide areas it can hide in during the day. At night, it will forage for food. When not seeking food at night, it beds down here.

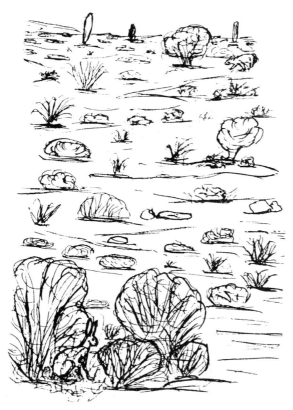

Jackrabbits' young are born here in the form nest. The nest is above ground, surrounded by tall grass. Several litters are born each year. The young at birth have hair and their eyes are open. They also begin hopping right away.

During the day, the jackrabbit sits in a form. It surveys the area all around the form. It spots predators while still a distance away. If the predator comes closer, the jackrabbit lays its ears down on its back. It crouches down in the form so as not to be seen. Suppose the predator spots the jackrabbit. It heads for the form. Out comes the jackrabbit! With a leap, it is off and running.

The predator is in close pursuit. Then the jackrabbit increases its speed. Jackrabbits can outrun most predators.

The jackrabbit's hind legs and feet are made for long distance running. They can cover some distance before tiring. They survive through flight. They will out distance the predator. It then rests in one of its forms. Jackrabbits run in circles in their territories. Predators may be unable to catch a jackrabbit on the run. However, a predator might lie in wait for the jackrabbit. It can ambush the jackrabbit on its regularly traveled paths.

Jackrabbits are most active late in the afternoon and at night. A jackrabbit eats grasses, leaves and twigs. Standing on its hind legs, it will cut off and eat any branch it can reach. Twigs and leaves of the Mesquite and Creosote Bush are favorite foods. Jackrabbits also eat pricklypear cacti. The cactus pads provide them with water.

Jackrabbit ears are very important at night. When foraging for food, they give notice of a predator's presence. Here is a sketch of a jackrabbit's ear.

Notice the long, wide-open area of the ear. That opening does not always face forward. No, the opening can be turned. The jackrabbit faces the opening toward a sound.

The ears are scanning devices. The ears are constantly twitching when feeding. The ears work independently of one another. One ear can be hearing in one direction. The other ear might be picking up sounds from another direction. They scan all directions for the slightest sound. So the jackrabbit's ears are very important when foraging for food at night. The ears give advance notice of predators. Many times this helps the jackrabbit slip away undetected. But at times, the jackrabbit is suddenly confronted by a predator.

The jackrabbit will leap away.

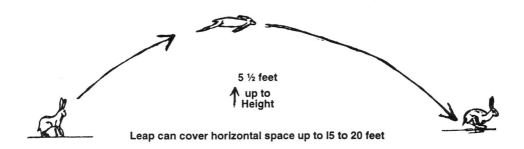

5 ½ feet
↑ up to
Height

Leap can cover horizontal space up to 15 to 20 feet

A startled jackrabbit can leap from two to five and a half feet into the air. In a one step leap, it can land some fifteen to twenty feet away. It is an expert at starting instantaneously. Soon it reaches full speed. The Blacktail Jackrabbit can go forty miles per hour. There is little vegetation in its way in the desert. Its best protection is speed. It runs, twists, leaps and dodges any pursuing predator. The jackrabbit will head for the nearest dense thicket. Down go its ears as it slips into a thicket. Few predators try entering a dense thicket.

The jackrabbit's ears are very efficient. They can pick up the slightest sound. The ears are laid back when running or hiding.

Let me tell you about the jackrabbit's eyes. Notice the eyes are placed on each side of the head. Each eye sees the area it is facing. In addition, the eyes bulge out from the head. The eyes now see what is in front, what is in back, and what is in the air above the animal. In essence, a jackrabbit with those two eyes, sees everything all around it.

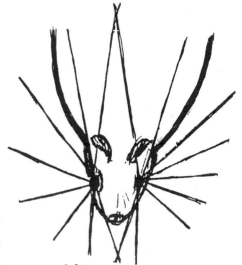

The jackrabbit eats plants. It is a herbivore. Animals that eat plants are herbivores. Herbivores have eyes like the jackrabbit. They must be vigilant. They must keep watch for predators. So their eyes register views all around them. Herbivores are food for flesh-eating

predators. Animals that eat other animals are called carnivores. They cannot see all around. They are like me, Creosote Charlie. They just see what is in front of them.

Carnivores' eyes face forward on the head. They are not on the sides as in the herbivores. They are looking ahead. They are stalking their prey.

Jackrabbit ears also help keep the animal cool. Say, it is a very hot day. Say, the j a c k r a b b i t becomes hot. It must lose some of this body heat. Here is how it does this. In each ear there are very, many blood vessels. These vessels lie close to the surface of the ear. Heated blood moves through these dilated vessels. Heat rays radiate from the blood and pass to the outside air.

As more and more heat is radiated to the air, the jackrabbit becomes cooler. The ears act like "radiators".

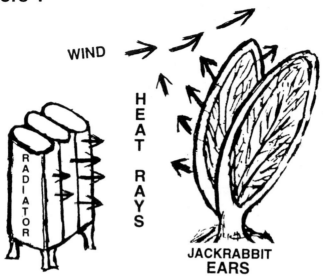

Well, my friend, those are a few interesting aspects of those jackrabbits. Many jackrabbits are produced each year. The ears, eyes, and those hind legs all help keep jackrabbits alive. However, many jackrabbits fall prey to predators. Many carnivores depend on some jackrabbit food.

Well, I must be going, Roscoe. Thanks, Creosote Charlie! We have learned much about those jackrabbits. Goodbye, Roscoe and friend! Goodbye, Creosote Charlie!

Photo by Earle A. Robinson

Look at that Western Bluebird over there, my friend. It will spot an insect below its perch. Down it will go to catch the insect.The bluebirds feed on insects, worms, berries, and fruit.

These   Western   Bluebirds   breed   from   British Columbia, Canada down to the mountains of Mexico. They are found in our western states.

There it flies away!

There is Ebenezer up ahead.   Ebenezer, will you tell our friend about the Desert Tortoise? Hi, Roscoe!

This is Desert Tortoise territory, my friend. This sandy, gravelly soil is ideal for making a tortoise den. There might be a tortoise nearby. Let's look!

Look over here! That is a land turtle, my friend, a tortoise.

Photo by Arizona Game and Fish Dept.

Notice its stocky legs. Those front legs are flattened. They are covered with scales. The toes are not webbed. The tortoise uses those legs like shovels. They are ideal for digging out a burrow. The hind legs are stumpy-shaped, like an elephant leg. The head is small and rounded in front. Scales cover the head, neck, and legs.

The tortoise has a bony shell. The shell has two main parts. The tall dome-shaped part covers the animal's back side. The flat part encloses the "belly" side.

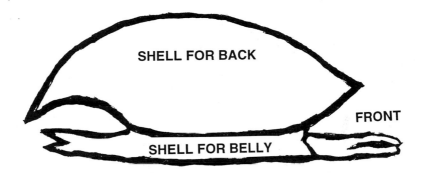

SHELL FOR BACK

FRONT

SHELL FOR BELLY

The two shells are connected along each side. The tortoise can pull its head, neck, and hind legs back into the shell. The front legs block off the front opening. All the openings are then closed. This gives the tortoise protection from many animals.

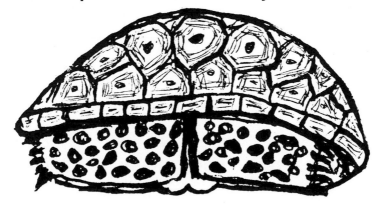

Look at this picture, my friend. It shows part of the bony top shell. It also shows the horny plates that cover the tortoise shell. These plates are very thin. One can see the growth lines on the individual plates. The horny plate is like our fingernail material. This shell covering helps camouflage the tortoise. It also helps the animal retain body moisture. It keeps the tortoise from drying out on hot, dry days. The head, neck, legs and tail are covered with scales. This also helps the tortoise retain body moisture.

In the springtime and early summer, the tortoise is up and about all day. It can walk twenty feet in one minute. It can do this if it doesn't stop for plant food.

The tortoise forages, it looks for food. Grasses are eaten. It also dines on other plants. It eats cactus fruits and desert flowers, too. It shreds its food.

The tortoise is especially active in rainy weather. It drinks water from rain puddles. It stores water in two sacs. These sacs lie under the  top shell. When the summer heat begins, the tortoise forages in early morning and late afternoon. In hot weather, it might not come out at all. If it forages, it will do so at night. During the heat of the day, the tortoise rests under bushes or in a burrow.

The tortoise spends the winter in its den. It retires for the winter in October or November. The den is usually a long burrow, eight to fifteen feet long. It digs out the den by using one front leg and then the other. They are excellent "shovels". First, it loosens some dirt. Then, it turns around and pushes the dirt out. Look at this sketch. Notice, the lower shell has turned upwards in the throat region. It serves very well as a bulldozer to move the den dirt.   The den opening and the tunnel is oval in shape.   The den usually has enlarged chambers. It will rest here during the winter. The Desert Tortoise also has some shallow burrows in its territory. These are about three to four feet long and slope downward. It rests in these shallow burrows when it is out foraging for food. These also serve as a cool, ideal retreat from the heat of the sun.

Well, my friend, we must be on our way. Thanks, Ebenezer, for telling us about the Desert Tortoise. Goodbye, Roscoe and friend!

CHAPTER TWELVE
CACTUS PETE AND THE BEAVERTAIL CACTUS

Cactus Pete is over there. He is looking at a cactus. Hi, Cactus Pete! Hi, Roscoe! Come over here, Roscoe. You must see these beautiful cactus flowers.

Look at those rose colored flowers. Aren't they beautiful? They certainly are, Cactus Pete. That is the Beavertail Cactus, Roscoe.

Notice the shape of the sections of the Beavertail Cactus, Roscoe. Each has a shape like a Beaver's tail.   This cactus belongs to a large group of cacti called prickly pear cacti. All cacti in this group have branches called pads. One

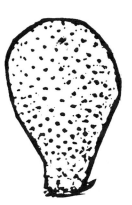

pad grows from another pad. This cactus is a many branched prickly pear. Inside each prickly pear pad is a network of fibers. The fibers help maintain the shape of the pad. Notice the network of fibers this pad had. The outside cover of the pad is gone.

Notice how smooth the side surface of those pads is. After rainy weather prickly pear pads bulge. They become filled with water. The cacti store water in their pads. The stored water will help the cactus grow and live in dry periods. As the water is used  by the plants, the two sides of the pad move closer together. Often one observes wrinkled pads in the desert. Wrinkled pads have lost much of their water. They are in the process of drying out.

Look at the flowers of that cactus. Notice the flowers are coming off the top edge of the pads. Some flowers are in full bloom. Others will soon be blooming. We find this cactus blooming in March or even later. The flowers will be pollinated by insects. A velvety fruit is produced. The fruit, when mature, is globular in shape. These fruits are edible and quite juicy. However, one must peel the fruit. Beware of the bristles on the outside covering of those fruits. They are small. The sides of these pads also have many small bristles. They stick in one's skin. So, be careful.

My friend, let me tell you how one recognizes a cactus plant. All cacti produce a structure called an areole. No other plants have these structures. So if a plant has areoles, it is a cactus. What are these areoles, you ask? Here is a sketch of some areoles. All of the dots on those cactus pads are areoles. An areole is a raised structure. It is a small "bump" on a cactus. There are two parts to an areole; two buds.

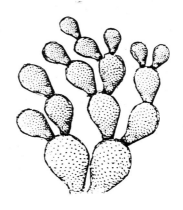

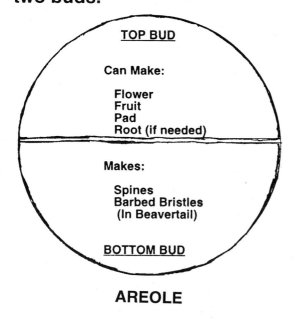

TOP BUD

Can Make:

Flower
Fruit
Pad
Root (if needed)

Makes:

Spines
Barbed Bristles
(In Beavertail)

BOTTOM BUD

AREOLE

The top bud can make a cactus section, or a flower and its fruit, or even a root. The bottom bud of an areole can make spines.

Areoles are located in different areas on different cacti. This Beavertail cactus belongs to a large group of cacti. They are called prickly pear cacti. In prickly pear cacti, areoles are always found on the edges and sides of a pad.

Look at the areoles on the side of this pad. They are raised structures. Each areole has two buds. The bottom bud on the pad side produces spines. Nothing is produced on the sides of a pad by the top part of the areole in the prickly pear cacti.

Here is a picture of an edge of a prickly pear pad. Notice the areoles. Spines have been produced by the lower part of an areole. The raised area by a spine is the top bud. A flower, fruit, or even a root can be produced from this bud on the edges of prickly pear cacti.

This picture shows a yellow flower growing from a top bud on the cactus pad edge. Two spines, below the flower, come from the lower bud of the areole.

This picture shows fruit on the edge of a prickly pear pad. There were five flowers there. Insects pollinated the flowers. Now the fruits with seeds are developing.

The upper buds on this pad edge had produced flowers. The fruits produced are now also gone. One can see the enlarged area of the areole where they were attached. New pads could be formed from these top buds. They had produced flowers, then fruits. Now, they could produce cactus pads. The spines from the lower buds are still there.

In our Beavertail Cactus, areoles are on the pad's edges and sides. Pads, spines, flowers, fruits, and even roots can develop on pad edges. No flowers, fruits, or pads are produced on the sides of pads. In the Beavertail the bottom part of areoles on the pad sides produces only small barbed bristles.

So, my friend, I have told you a very basic thing about our cacti. All plants in our desert that have areoles are cacti. No other plants have this structure, an areole. The next time we meet, my friend, I will tell you more.

Now, I must be off to my cactus garden. Did you know that I grow cacti?   Yes, Cactus Pete has quite a cactus garden.   We will see it in our travels.
Goodbye, Cactus Pete!
Goodbye, Roscoe!   Goodbye, my friend!

Photo by Earle A. Robinson

My friend, look at this Elf Owl. It is small - just five to six inches long. It was out at night, foraging for food. It caught something. It lives in the Saguaro Cactus.

CHAPTER THIRTEEN
HORATIO AND PHAINOPEPLA & MISTLETOE

My friend, come over here. We have some young birds in a nest. See there is the nest. It is built on the palo verde branch. Oh, we are lucky. Here comes one of the adult birds. The

Photo by Earle A. Robinson

young bird opens its mouth wide. It receives one mistletoe berry. That was swallowed, another berry is needed. So, the adult drops another berry into that open mouth. Look, that adult has more berries.

Where are all the berries coming from? As if by magic, more berries appear in the beak of the adult bird. Let me make some sketches for you. The sketches will help you understand what is happening here. Say early in the morning, this adult bird goes out to secure some food. It picks some Mistletoe berries. It swallows these berries. The berries go down the food tube to the stomach. The bird has obtained its food.

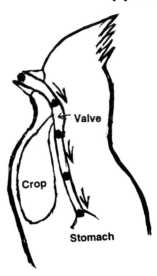

Eating

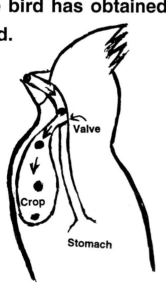

Filling Crop

It now closes the tube to the stomach. It opens the tube to the crop. Now it must secure food for the young in the nest. The crop is now filled with Mistletoe berries. Back to the nest the bird goes.

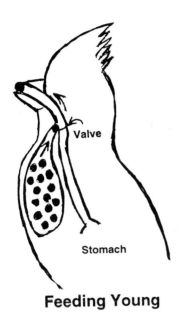

Valve

Stomach

Feeding Young

Now berries, one by one, are brought back up to the beak. Muscles in the crop and tube move the berries up to the beak. One by one, the berries are given to the young. The young have now received their first food today. Later they will be needing more food.

Here comes Horatio, my friend. Hi, Horatio! Hi, Roscoe! I see you have also found the Phainopepla's nest. I have been watching this nest for some days.

These birds are very interesting. They don't stay here all year. This pair migrated back in late fall. It set up its territory.

The Phainopepla's territory includes some trees having large Mistletoe plants. There is enough food here for the pair to live and raise young. Other Phainopeplas will be driven out of this area. You can see the Mistletoe berries are now ripe. The nest, notice, is built in the palo verde plant. Around May the Mistletoe berry season will end. Then the Phainopeplas will leave our Sonoran Desert. Some will migrate east, some north, and some west.

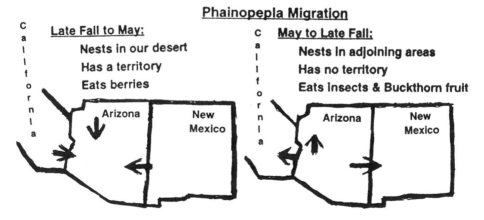

Phainopepla Migration

Late Fall to May:
 Nests in our desert
 Has a territory
 Eats berries

May to Late Fall:
 Nests in adjoining areas
 Has no territory
 Eats insects & Buckthorn fruit

In the summer, these new areas will be cooler. There will be abundant insect food. They will again nest and raise young. In their summer homes, they do not set up territories. In late fall or early winter, these birds migrate back to our desert. The Hackberry fruit is now available. The Mistletoe berries are ripening. So the birds come back here for a warmer winter stay.

In one area, the Phainopepla live off berries. In the other area, their main food is insects. They establish a territory in one area. No territory is established in the other. They nest and raise young in both winter and summer areas. This, my friend, is indeed an interesting bird.

Look at those Mistletoe plants in that palo verde tree. There are four Mistletoe plants in that tree. Those plants are parasites. They are living off that palo verde tree.

You might wonder how the Mistletoe plants got in this tree. Let me tell you about that.
The male Phainopepla often sits in the top of this tree. It will survey its territory. These birds eat the Mistletoe berries.
Each berry has several seeds inside the fruit. The fruit is digested. It is food for the bird.The seeds are not digested. High in the tree, the bird droppings fall down toward the ground. On the way down, some droppings may hit the palo verde branches.   All Mistletoe seeds have a sticky material around the seeds. The sticky seeds cling to a branch.

The seed will now germinate. It will grow. First the seed coat is broken. The cells inside multiply. They make the miniature mistletoe plant. These plant cells break down the palo verde bark there.

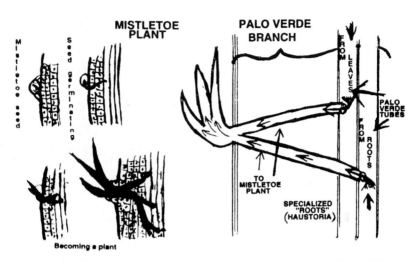

This small Mistletoe plant makes specialized "roots". These "roots" are now inside the palo verde branch. The ends of these "roots" connect into the conducting tubes of the tree. The tree conducts water and other nutrients in its tubes. The small plant now absorbs - drains away - these materials from the tree tubes. The water and inorganic materials now go into the Mistletoe plant. It grows and grows. Given large Mistletoe plants in its branches, a tree may die.

The scientific name for the Mistletoe plant is Phoradendron. Phora comes from a Greek word which means thief. Dendron comes from a Greek word which means tree. So the name for the Mistletoe plant is tree thief. That is exactly what the Mistletoe is.

The Mistletoe plant is composed of twigs. There are no leaves on the plant. The plant grows into large clusters of stems - twigs. The plant has male flowers on one tree. Female flowers are found on another tree. The flowers appear in the spring. They are tiny, yellow green in color. They are fragrant. They attract bees and insects.   Female flowers once pollinated form seeds in berries. At first they are greenish-white berries.

These berries turn to a red color when the fruit is mature. The berries are taken by the adult birds to the nest for the young. Fruit is edible and surrounds several sticky seeds.   So the Phainopeplas help distribute the seeds of this plant.

We often see that shiny black bird sitting in the top of trees. One wonders why they don't get too hot up there in the sun. It seems strange, but the black color seems ideal in our desert. There are few white desert birds. Let me make a sketch for you. The rays of the sun heat up the black feathers. This heat is not passed to the skin and body of the bird.

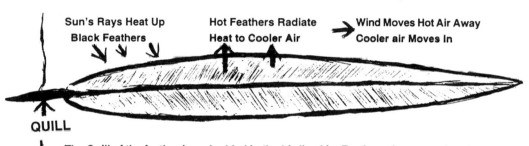

Sun's Rays Heat Up Black Feathers

Hot Feathers Radiate Heat to Cooler Air

Wind Moves Hot Air Away Cooler air Moves In

QUILL

The Quill of the feather is embedded in the bird's skin. Feathers do not touch skin. Heat would have to move down the quill of the feather into the body.

The feathers become hot. Heat is radiated from the feathers to the air. The air close to the feathers now becomes warmer.   In the process, the feather becomes cooler. Again the feather is warmed up. Again the feather radiates heat to the air. Once more the wind moves the warm air away. This process reduces the heat in the feathers.

Say the bird becomes hotter sitting there in the tree. The bird will change its position relative to the sun. The sun had been striking the side of the bird. Now the sun strikes the bird head-on. Even the tail-on rays will do. In these positions, the bird will absorb less heat. When it becomes really hot, the bird will head into the shade of a palo verde or mesquite tree.

Well, I must be going now. Goodbye, Roscoe! Goodbye, Horatio! Thanks for telling us about the Phainopepla and the Mistletoe.

CHAPTER FOURTEEN
CREOSOTE CHARLIE AND THE
WESTERN DIAMONDBACK RATTLESNAKE

There's Creosote Charlie.

Hi,Charlie!

Take it easy, Roscoe! I have a Western Diamondback Rattlesnake over here. See it is heading for us.

Snakes have no legs.
But they say a rattler can crawl faster
than a man walks. So we will have to be careful!

Photo by George Olin

Do you hear that buzzing sound? That is the snake's rattle. That rattler is warning us: KEEP YOUR DISTANCE. Usually when disturbed, the snake coils itself into a spiral. You can see that is a large bodied snake. The head is very evident. It is broad and flat on top. Many snakes have round eyes. They are always open. There is a clear covering over the eye called the spectacle. The rattler's eyes look like slits. These snakes are most active at dusk and at night. When the snake is hunting, the slits are gone. The eyes are wide open.

Rattlers shed their skins. The outer part of the skin is shed. Even the covering of  the eye is shed. Here is how it is done. The skin around the mouth becomes loose. As the snake crawls, this is turned backwards.

As the snake crawls, more and more skin moves backwards. Before long, the entire skin is shed. In the process a horny skin part remains at the tail end. This becomes another section of the rattle.   These rattle parts are hollow. They are connected loosely with each other. They produce a sound when the tail is   vibrated. The number of rattles does not indicate age. It tells how many times the skin has been shed. Snakes shed skin several times a year. The 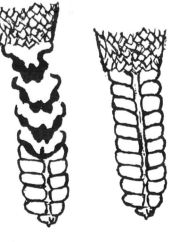 above snake shed its skin eleven times.

Rattlesnakes are Pit Vipers. All Pit Vipers have heat sensitive pits. The rattler's pits help it secure its food. A pit is a depression on the head. A pit lies between each eye and the nostril. So there are two pits, one on each side. Here is a sketch of the pit. The pit makes a chamber. This small chamber has a thin skin floor. Below this floor is another small

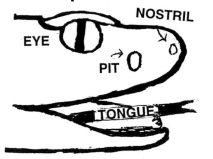

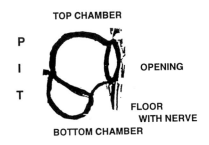

chamber. Fine nerve endings are in this floor. These endings are sensitive to heat rays. Here is how the pits work. A mouse moves in front of the rattler. The mouse is warm blooded. It gives off heat rays. The pits pick up these heat rays. The rattler moves its head. The pits zero in on the heat source.

The rattler now knows the animal's size and position. The rattler now strikes. It grabs the mouse.

This brings us to the subject of fangs. The rattlers have two curved fangs. One fang is on each side. The fangs lie back against the roof mouth. Each fang is like a hollow needle. Each has an opening close to the tip end. The snake opens its mouth wide. Muscles on each side swing the fangs forward. The fangs pierce the mouse skin. A poison gland is located on each side of the snake's head. Poison is stored there.

Now the poison is forced down through the hollow fangs into the animal. The rattler then releases the animal. The mouse might move a short distance. Soon it will collapse. The snake with its tongue, tracks the odor trail of the mouse. The rattler uses the heat sensitive pits to locate the mouse. The snake will locate the animal. It will swallow it - head first!

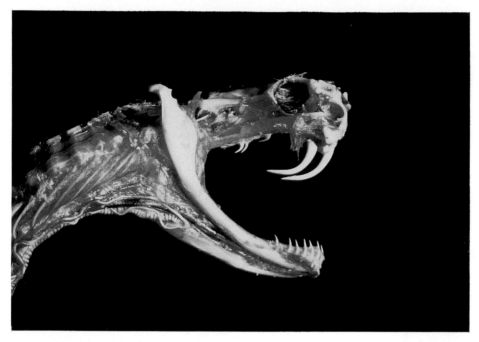

Photo by George Olin

Notice the fangs and teeth in this picture. The teeth make sure no prey can go back out of the mouth opening. This dried out snake head section also shows the fangs.

My friend, many snakes lay eggs. Rattlesnakes, however, bear live young. There are about nine young born each time, on an average. A young snake is about a foot long at birth. Rattlers prey on many animals. Mice, rats, rabbits, squirrels, birds, and lizards all are rattlesnake food. Well, I must be going, Roscoe. Watch that rattlesnake. We will, Creosote Charley. Thanks for telling us about that rattlesnake.

CHAPTER FIFTEEN
ROUNDTAIL GROUND SQUIRREL

Photo by George Olin

My friend, look at that Roundtail Ground Squirrel. It Is well named. It has a long, slender, round tail. Most squirrels have bushy tails. Not this squirrel, it has a round tail. Bushy tailed squirrels spend a great part of a day up in trees. Not the Roundtails. They spend most of their time on the ground. Many Bushy tailed squirrels have their homes in the trees. These Roundtails live in burrows underground. Except for these differences, the Roundtails are like all other squirrels.

Let's consider the Roundtail Ground Squirrel's underground burrow.

Look at those holes under those Creosote Bushes. There are many openings there. Those bushes have many intertwining roots underground. The Roundtail Squirrel and many other animals live underground there. All have constructed their burrows in the sand around these roots. The roots give structural support for their burrows. These animals know how to handle the desert heat. They live underground.

Having a home in the ground has advantages in the desert. Notice these temperature differences.They were recorded from a burrow. No wonder these squirrels have taken to living

Desert Temperatures on Hot Days
Air   temperature--------103 degrees
Soil temperature ------155 degrees

Burrow Temperature on Hot Days
Inside entrance----------------90 degrees
Two feet underground------86 degrees

Night temperatures
Winter air temperature--
        can go below------------40 degrees
Winter burrow temperature--
        about------------70 degrees

underground. It is one way to beat the desert heat in the day and the cold at night.

The Roundtail Ground Squirrels mate in the spring. About twenty-seven days later the young are born. There are usually from three to nine young in a litter. The squirrels are active all year in some areas. In other areas, they hibernate during the winter months.

Many animals prey on these squirrels. Hawks, eagles, coyotes, foxes, badgers, and bobcats will try to catch them. Snakes also enter their burrows looking for squirrel food.

Like other squirrels, the Roundtails are herbivores. They eat plant food. Seeds and nuts are their basic foods. When these are not available, they eat green plants. They will also climb into Ironwood trees for seeds. They eat tender buds on the Creosote Bush branches.

In the cool mornings, the Roundtails come out of their burrows. They forage for food until it becomes hot.

During the heat of the summer days, the squirrel heads for its burrow. Here it rests and keeps cool. On the hot days, it will come out again in late afternoon. It will forage in this cooler air.

Predators catch many Roundtail Ground Squirrels. However, some will always live through the winter and raise new litters next year. Enough new squirrels are produced each year.

Well, my friend, let's be on our way.

CHAPTER SIXTEEN
EBENEZER AND THE HORNED LIZARD

Hi, Roscoe! Hi, Ebenezer! Here we find you just when we need you. We have been looking for a Horned Lizard. I said, "If Ebenezer were here, he would find a Horned Lizard." Oh, Roscoe, I think we might be able to find one. Let's see, that lizard might be sunning itself on a rock. No, it's too hot right now. Then, it is probably out looking for food. Horned Lizards' main food is ants. Perhaps we can find one near an ant nest. Let's look for an ant nest. Over here, Ebenezer. Here are some ants. There is a lineup of ants. Oh, I think I see that lizard. See it there. It's about to capture some ants.

The Horned Lizard has a sticky tongue. With one swipe, the lizard has four or five ants. It won't eat too many. It could eat all the ants in that nest. But then, there would be no ants for the next day. That lizard is a prudent predator. It looks forward to many future colony ant meals. So, it doesn't eat too many today.

Photo by George Olin

Look at that Horned Lizard. Notice, it has a very flattened body. It has many spines. On the back of the head, those spines look like daggers. The sharp scales all face outwards. It has a short tail. Those are features that describe that lizard.

One finds these lizards in flat areas of sand and gravel. It lives in areas with Creosote Bushes, Sagebrush, and Saltbush plants. It prefers areas with low shrubs. When frightened, the lizard scoots under the low branches of these shrubs. If a rodent burrow is available, it will hide in it. In our area, the female lays eggs in June and July. A female lizard lays from several to as many as sixteen eggs.

The Horned Lizard blends in well with the surface it is on. It blends in well because it can change the color of its back. This ability helps the lizard in several important ways.

First, it helps the lizard maintain a good body temperature. Say the lizard is cold. It will darken the color of its wide back. Now, more of the sun's rays are absorbed. This heats up the lizard.

Say the lizard is too hot. It must become cooler. Now, it makes its back lighter in color. More of the sun's rays are reflected. The lizard becomes cooler. This lizard regulates its body temperature by changing its color. This ability helps the lizard maintain a needed body temperature. This ability also helps keep many Horned Lizards alive. So well, in fact, that many predators do not notice them. On a dark background, the lizard becomes darker. Say it scampers to a lighter background. In a few minutes, its back will become lighter in color. It will look very much like the surface there. So, this ability also protects the animal.

The Horned Lizard is a very unusual animal. When it wants to go underground, it proceeds in a very novel way. Let me tell you about that.

Some animals dig out a burrow. They do it head-first. The front paws and legs are efficient digging structures. Other animals dig out a burrow tail-first. The paws and legs of the hind feet of these animals do the digging. They are also good at making a burrow.

How does the Horned Lizard go underground? It also digs its way underground. It digs out an underground spot - "belly"-first. Recall, you saw this lizard had a very flat shape. Well, it uses its sides like shovels.

It tilts its sides like shovels. It tilts its body sideways. It shoves its side into the sand. It flips the sand, on that side, up on its back. Quickly, it tilts its body. It shoves the other tilted side into the sand. It flips this sand up on its back. It keeps doing this, one side, then the other side. It keeps sinking deeper into the sand. The sand now covers the lizard.

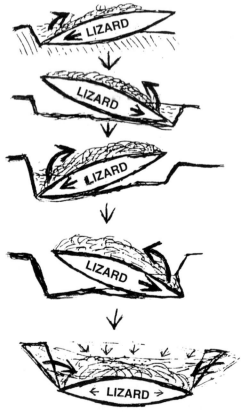

The Horned Lizard will go underground if it is too warm. There are no hot sun's rays underground. It is cooler there. It also buries itself to escape predators. It also buries itself when it wants to rest.

The Horned Lizard has additional ways to protect itself. When caught, it gulps in large amounts of air. It inflates. In the process it also jabs, what is grasping it, with its horns.

A Horned Lizard can also squirt blood from its eyes. In the lizard head, there is a space behind the eye. This is filled with blood. This space connects with the eyelid. A pore is located on the eyelid. Muscles contract around the blood-filled space. This squirts blood out through the pore on the eyelid. The blood squirts several feet. This action seems to be protective in nature; to repel a predator

The Horned Lizard eats insects, spiders, and berries. In turn, it is food for Road Runners, shrikes, hawks, and coyotes. The Horned Lizard is quite an animal! Well, I must be going. Goodbye, Roscoe! Goodbye, my friend!   Goodbye, Ebenezer!

CHAPTER SEVENTEEN
GILROY AND THE PIPEVINE SWALLOWTAIL

Oh, Gilroy is up ahead. He is looking at something. Hi, Gilroy! Hi, Roscoe! Come see this Pipevine Swallowtail, Roscoe. Notice that it has large wings. It had long tails on the hind wings. I see that one has b e e n broken off. This is called the P i p e v i n e Swallowtail. T h o s e white spots really show up against a solid bluegreen color. Many

Photo by Earle A. Robinson

swallowtails have colors that contrast like this. One finds white and black, or, yellow and black.

Photo by Earle A. Robinson

The butterfly has just turned around on that plant. Now we see the underside of its wings. They are certainly different from the color on the top side. One would never expect this difference in color between two sides of a butterfly's wing.

This butterfly lays eggs on Pipevine plants. The caterpillar that hatches from the egg is black. Red spots on each side line its back. Near the tail, the

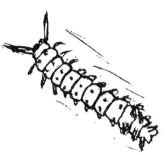

caterpillar has three projections on each side. The caterpillar, when mature, changes into a chrysalis.

Here is a sketch of the chrysalis. Let me explain how this happens. The caterpillar plcks a spot for this change. It attaches its rear end to a stem by a silken pad. Then it constructs a "girdle". You can see how the "girdle" holds the chrysalis head-up on the stem. One end of the "girdle" is attached to the stem on one side. The silk "girdle" passes over the middle of the chrysalis. The other end of the "girdle is attached to the stem on the other side. The caterpillar changes its shape into the shape of this chrysalis.

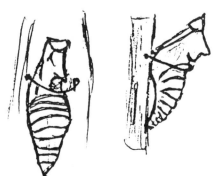

The caterpillar's head-end area will become the butterfly's head-end area. In this stage, one sees little change on the outside. But inside, change is going on. All caterpillar parts are being recycled. They are recycled into a butterfly. All caterpillar parts are being used. No new materials are needed. What was a wormlike caterpillar comes out a dainty butterfly. This, my friend, is amazing. This is a real recycling setup.

One wonders. Are all butterflies produced in this same way? Do all have a silken "girdle"? Do all chrysalis stages hang head-up on the stem? Well, no. Many butterflies have a chrysalis like the Buckeye Butterfly. There is no silken "girdle". One is not needed. The chrysalis hangs head-down on the stem. The same perfect recycling takes place. Nature does not need uniformity in all its processes. No, variety is still the spice of life.

My friend, this Pipevine Swallowtail is interesting in another way. The female butterflies lay eggs on Pipevine plants. The caterpillars eat the leaves of these plants. Pipevine plants have a toxin in their leaves. This discourages many animals from eating the leaves. The Pipevine caterpillar doesn't mind. It eats the leaves. The toxin now is in the caterpillar. The caterpillar changes into a butterfly. Now the butterfly has the toxin in its tissues. Birds dine on butterflies. Tasting one Pipevine Swallowtail is almost too much. Because of the toxin, birds will not try eating another Pipevine Swallowtail. That is fine for the Pipevine Swallowtail.

Another butterfly also benefits living in our area. It is the Red-spotted Purple. Here is a picture of it.

The Red-spotted Purple looks very much like the Pipevine Swallowtail. Its bright blue wings resemble the wings of the Pipevine Swallowtail.

The underside of the wings of this butterfly has bright orange spots. The Pipevine Swallowtail also has orange spots. So the undersides look very much alike. One look at this butterfly by a bird will be enough. Birds that have tried eating a Pipevine Swallowtail will avoid this butterfly. So the Red - spotted Purple benefits. That is very interesting, Gilroy. We enjoyed learning about these butterflies.

CHAPTER EIGHTEEN
THE CREOSOTE BUSH

Look at those shrubs up ahead, my friend.

Those bushes are all alike. That is the only evident plant in this area. The bushes extend back as far as one can see. Those, my friend, are Creosote Bushes. It is the most abundant plant on plains and slopes in this part of our desert. It is said that this plant covers more desert space than any other plant. After a rain, the Creosote Bush gives off an odor. The odor has a creosote-smell to it. Here, take one of the leaves. Break the leaf in half with your fingers. Now smell the broken halves. It smells like creosote, doesn't it? That is why it is named the Creosote Bush.

There are many branches arising from the base of the bush. Those are long stems. As you see, this is not a dense bush. The Creosote Bush has a root system like the Saguaro Cactus. Roots extend down into the soil that anchor the bush. The vertical roots go down some depth. Many smaller roots radiate

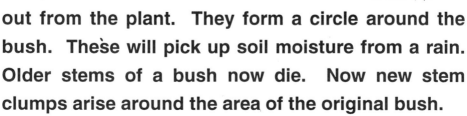

out from the plant. They form a circle around the bush. These will pick up soil moisture from a rain. Older stems of a bush now die. Now new stem clumps arise around the area of the original bush.

As this goes on above ground, more roots are made underground. This spreading system of roots is found in desert areas. Soil is effectively tied down in this root system. In our desert, plants develop a radial root system that reflects the rainfall in the area. Here is a picture of Creosote Bushes. They are growing rather close together.

The radial root system is like in this sketch. Each plant has a system that will provide the plant with enough water.

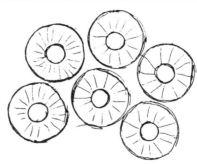

Here is another picture of Creosote Bushes.

Notice these bushes are farther. This area has less yearly rainfall than the other area. So the plants have to expand the area of the radial root system. The radial root system of these bushes would be like in this sketch. The principle on the radial root system for many desert plants is: plants closer together, more rain water every year; plants farther apart, less rain water every year. Desert plants show this adaptability regarding radial root systems. Rainfall, my friend, helps space Creosote Bushes.

My friend, notice no plants grow between those Creosote Bushes. There is just so much water here. Any new Creosote Bush growing in among these bushes would take water from these bushes. So the plant produces a substance that in the soil makes it impossible for another Creosote Bush to grow there. Again, these plants space themselves in an area. Looking at an area that is entirely Creosote Bushes makes one wonder if it is not an orchard that has been planted there.

The Creosote Bush cannot store water like a cactus. When it rains, the bush takes in water. It uses this water sparingly. Very little moisture is given off to the dry desert air. The leaves are small in size. Most plants this size have larger leaves. The small leaf size helps the plant cope with the water and heat problems of the desert. Leaves are also coated with a varnish-like substance. This reduces water loss from the leaves. The shiny coat of varnish-like material also reflects some of the sun's rays. This helps regulate the plant temperature. Leaves also control how much leaf surface faces the sun's rays. The leaves turn so that very little of the leaf surface faces the sun's rays.

Leaflets of the leaves fold
together. This also helps
conserve water and reduce
heat problems.   During
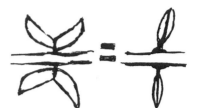
drought periods, a bush makes smaller and tougher
leaves. Leaves and twigs may be shed during hot, dry
periods. This way the bush saves water and copes
with desert heat. After drought periods the bush may
look like a bunch of dried out sticks.

Given late fall rains, or spring weather, everything
changes. New green stems are made. Leaves are
produced.   Each leaf has two parts; two leaflets
attached at the base. Leaves are opposite one
another. Flowers are not long in appearing.

The bush becomes covered with bright yellow flowers. Bees and insects leave their nests and burrows. They come to the flowers for nectar and pollen. Scales at the base of the stamens are the flowers' nectaries. Flowers last a few hours to a day.

Once the flower is pollinated, a fruit is produced. Fruits are globe-shaped. They are covered with a fine, white, hair-like covering. Each has the former style of the flower attached to it.

Quail, doves, finches, and sparrows eat the seeds and fruit of the Creosote Bush. The Chuckwalla lizard eats the leaves of the bush. Harvester ants take the Creosote leaves underground. They are used in growing their mushrooms.

Some insects live only in these Creosote Bushes. Here is a picture of a Creosote Bush Grasshopper.

Praying Mantis and Cricket also live in the Creosote Bushes. There is a Creosote Gall Midge that forms these leaf galls. This midge is a fly. It looks like a mosquito. A midge egg on a leaf hatches into a larva. It eats some of the leaf. Then it secretes a substance into the leaf tissue. This induces plant growth around the larva. This growth is the gall that you see on that branch. The larva inside eats the gall tissue.It eventually changes into a mature midge.

The Creosote Bush also serves as "landlord" to many desert animals. The radial and deep roots hold down the desert sand.   As stems of the bush die, new clumps are produced.   So, underground there is a veritable tangle of vertical and horizontal roots. All the plant roots tie down the sand. This makes an ideal place for an animal burrow. Many animals take

 advantage of this. They make burrows under these bushes. The root system p r o v i d e s s t r u c t u r a l support for their b u r r o w s . G r o u n d s q u i r r e l s , l i z a r d s , kangaroo rats, snakes, toads, tarantulas, spiders, geckos, - even birds, live in these burrows.

Well, we must be on our way, my friend.

Hi, Gilroy! Oh, Hi, Roscoe! Come look at this ant nest. That is a large opening, Gilroy. Tell my friend about ants. We have so many here in our desert. I would be happy to do that, Roscoe.

My friend, ants are insects. Insects have a skeleton on the outside. Here, let me make a drawing of an ant.

I will cut the body in half. Then you can understand how it's made. There are three sections to an insect's body. An ant has three body sections; head, thorax, and abdomen.

ABDOMEN	THORAX	HEAD
Digestive System	Jointed legs	Eyes
Crop	Wings - male	Antennae
Reproductive parts	and female	Mouth parts
Scent gland		Brain

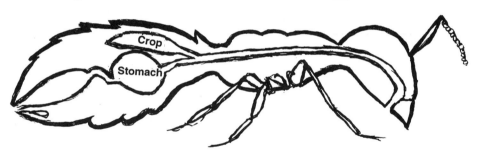

The first body part is the head. The head has eyes in it. Two antennae come off the front of the head. Ant antennae are bent. That is how you can tell ants from other insects. All insects have antennae. Only ants have bent antennae. The mouth parts are located in the head. Ants have powerful jaws. The brain is located in the head.

The middle part of an ant is called the thorax. The jointed legs and wings, if present, are attached to this section of the body. Many muscles are located in the thorax area. The muscles contract and make the legs and wings move.

The last body part is called the abdomen. Note I have put in the food tube. It starts at the mouth and continues as a tube through the thorax. In the abdomen a side branch is called a crop. This is a dead end bag. Liquid food is stored here. Ants feed young and one another. In doing this, food from the crop is used. The food tube continues on to the stomach. Here food is digested. Waste products pass through a short intestine. This empties into a larger space with an opening at the abdomen tip. A stinger with its poison gland and scent gland are also located here.

ANT FEEDING LARVA
using food from its crop.

Ants have powerful jaws. Ants use their jaws in digging. Chambers are dug under the ground for the nest. The ant jaws break down the ground into small pieces. The ant then carries these pieces above ground. It drops them over the rim side of the funnel opening. The black ants are doing that in this picture.

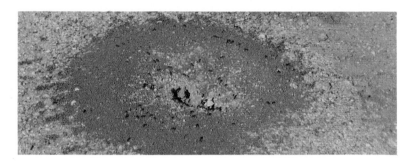

Ants also use their jaws in fighting. Jaws are strong weapons. They are used in fighting other ants and insects. Jaws are also useful in carrying things. Food is carried back to a nest in jaws. Jaws are used in moving larvae and pupae to a new space in the ant colony quarters.

ANTS USING JAWS FOR CARRYING THINGS

Jaws of different kinds of ants become specialized.

In Carpenter Ants, the jaws cut wood into small pieces. These pieces are then swallowed and digested. The Carpenter Ants eat wood.

In Harvester Ants, the jaws bite into hard seed coats. They cut away the covering over their seed food.

In Fungus Ants, the sharp jaws cut pieces out of leaves. These pieces will serve as food for growing mushroom food in the nest.

Now, let me tell you about ant colonies. My friend, ants are terrestrial. They live in and on the ground. There are no solitary ants. All ants live in colonies. How is an ant colony formed?
I knew you would ask me that.
Here is how an ant colony
gets started. In spring,
an existing ant colony
produces winged
females and males.
The males mate with the females.

Now the fertilized female seeks a spot to start an ant colony. Depending on the kind of ant, rotten wood or a space in the soil will do. The female finds the spot. Then it breaks off its wings. Wings will not be needed anymore.

The queen now sets about laying eggs.

The eggs hatch into larvae. The larvae have no legs. They are fed the food from the ant's crop.

The larvae change into pupae. In this stage, they do not eat. Slowly the wormlike grub changes into an ant. All these ants are females.

They are the workers in the colony. They wait on the queen. They feed and groom the queen. The queen lays more eggs. The female workers feed the larvae.

You know, in wasp and bee colonies, the young are reared in separate cells. This is not so with ants. Ant larvae lie on the floor of the ant chamber. As the colony grows larger, new galleries and chambers are made. The 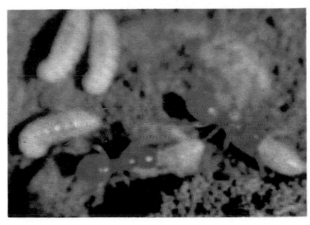 larvae are moved from one chamber to another. Larvae and pupae are moved often in a colony.

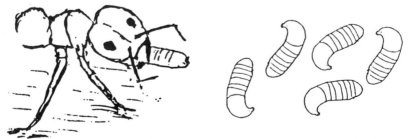

As the colony grows, female workers patrol the area around the nest looking for food. Ants feed on many things. Ants eat wood, seeds, other insects, fungi, nectar and scale insects.

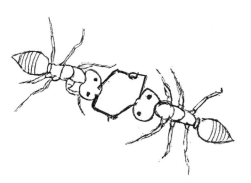

Ants of a colony touch one another's antennae when meeting. Eggs and larvae also receive attention. They are constantly licked. Ants exchange food with one another. This appears to help solidify the bond of colony members.

Ants lay down scent trails. Say, an ant finds food. There is much food there. The ant carries some food back to the nest. As it goes back to the nest, it marks

a trail from the food source. It touches the tip of its abdomen to the ground. A small amount of scent is deposited on the ground. It does this all the way back to the nest. Now a scent trail has been made from the nest to the source.

BRINGING GRASS BLADE TO THE NEST   LAYING THE SCENT TRAIL

Once the ant returns to the nest, it deposits the food. It touches the antennae of other ants. Now the ants set out for the food site. They will not have to spend time looking for it. It will be at the end of the scent trail. Scent trails don't last too long. They don't have to last long. As the ants set out from the nest, they reinforce the scent trail. Ants pick up this scent by receptors in their legs and antennae.

HEADING OUT TO THE FOOD SITE   REINFORCING THE SCENT TRAIL

As more ants are produced, remodeling goes on in the nest. The ants dig out dirt. New chambers and galleries are made. Colonies last for several years. Sometimes newly mated queens remain in a colony. They also lay eggs producing more ants in the colony. So a colony can last a long time. That is something about ants, my friend. The queens and workers are all females. Males are few in numbers and are not always present in a colony.

I must be going now. Later I will tell you about fungus growing ants. Goodbye, my friend! Goodbye, Roscoe.

My friend, will you look at that dragonfly. The sun has made its head into a "happy face". Imagine a dragon with a happy face.

You can't deny it. There is that dragon - and it has this "happy face".
Notice how the dragonfly is poised on top of that weed seed pod. It has two large eyes. They are brownish in color. It is looking at us. It has two pairs of wings. See how the wings are held straight out from the body. It always holds its wings outstretched when resting. It looks like an airplane. They dart here and there. They alter their flight direction gracefully with no problem. They are daytime fliers.

The white spot, below the eyes, is the front of the head. That dragon fly has biting parts on the bottom side of the head.

Look at those legs. They are not bent. They are extended out to their full length. One can count those legs. There are six legs. It uses its legs in capturing insects. It catches flies, butterflies, gnats, midges, and many other insects. It overtakes an insect on the wing. Its legs now form a basket. As it moves forward, it scoops up the insect into that leg basket. It will then proceed to eat the insect while it is still flying.

Or, the dragonfly could find a resting place like this weed seed stem to eat its food.

Seeing that dragonfly here tells me that there is water nearby. The adult dragonflies lay their eggs by rivers, lakes, and ponds. Eggs are placed on the water surface, on plants, or inserted into plant tissues. They hatch into a larval form called a nymph. The nymph's lower lip is hinged or elongated. It can be suddenly extended to seize its prey. When the lip is not being used, it fits over the face area somewhat like a mask. Well, there it goes. We'll probably see it again.

Well, my friend, we have come to the end of our travels together for today. I hope that you have enjoyed traveling with me. We have seen some interesting desert plants and animals, haven't we? However, we have just skimmed the surface. There are still so many other interesting desert animals and plants. You will have to travel with me again. In our future travels we will be seeing the Gila Monster, the Sonoran Coral Snake, the Road Runner, and desert bats, just to name a few desert animals.

You now know that our desert has many different kinds of plants. There are cacti of all shapes and sizes. In the spring our desert is one big carpet of beautiful spring flowers. You will enjoy seeing and knowing about these plants.These plants and animals cope with the desert conditions in interesting ways.

Our next book will have a real surprise in store for you. Did you know that real gold was mined in our Sonoran Desert? In book two of this desert series, Otis and Oswald will explain how gold was mined in the Vulture Gold Mine. So keep in touch, my friend.

TRACKING IT DOWN

Desert Animals

Ants	139-147
Bluebird, Western	80
Butterfly, Painted Lady	52
Butterfly, Pipevine	123-128
Butterfly, Red-spotted Purple	127-128
Dragonfly	148-150
Flicker, Gilded	27-32
Grasshopper, Creosote Bush	135
Grasshopper, Pallid-winged	33-40
Jackrabbit, Blacktail	71-90
Lizard, Horned	117-122
Owl, Elf	96
Phainopepla	97-106
Rattlesnake,	
Western Diamondback	107-112
Spider, Wolf	58
Squirrel, Roundtail Ground	113-116
Tortoise, Desert	81-86
Woodpecker, Gila	27-32
Woodrat	47-51
Wren, Cactus	53-57
Yucca Moth	65-70

Desert Plants

Brittlebush	59-63
Cactus, Beavertail	87-95
Cactus, Hedgehog	41-46
Cactus, Pincushion	64
Cactus, Saguaro	15-26
Creosote Bush	129-138
Mistletoe	97-106
Palo Verde	97-106
Yucca	65-70